FAMILIES AROUND THE WORLD

A family from
VIETNAM

Simon Scoones

RSVP

RAINTREE
STECK-VAUGHN
P U B L I S H E R S
The Steck-Vaughn Company

Austin, Texas

FAMILIES AROUND THE WORLD

A family from **BOSNIA**

A family from **BRAZIL**

A family from **CHINA**

A family from **ETHIOPIA**

A family from **GERMANY**

A family from **GUATEMALA**

A family from **IRAQ**

A family from **JAPAN**

A family from **SOUTH AFRICA**

A family from **VIETNAM**

The family featured in this book is an average Vietnamese family. The Nguyens were chosen because they are typical in terms of income, housing, number of children, and lifestyle.

Cover: The Nguyens outside their home with all their possessions
Title page: Canh carries crops picked in the fields near her home.
Contents page: Villagers cycle to their work in the paddy fields.

Picture Acknowledgments: All the photographs in this book were taken by Leong Ka Tai. The photographs were supplied by Material World/Impact Photos and were first published in 1994 by Sierra Club Books in Material World: A Global Family Portrait © Copyright Peter Menzel/Material World. The map artwork on page 4 was produced by Peter Bull.

Published by Raintree Steck-Vaughn Publishers, an imprint of Steck-Vaughn Company

Printed in Italy. Bound in the United States.
1 2 3 4 5 6 7 8 9 0 02 01 00 99 98

Library of Congress Cataloging-in-Publication Data
Scoones, Simon.
A family from Vietnam / Simon Scoones.
p. cm.—(Families around the world)
Includes bibliographical references and index.
Summary: Describes the activities of a family of five living in a small village in the north of Vietnam and provides information about their daily life and customs.
ISBN 0-8172-4908-7
1. Family—Vietnam—Juvenile literature.
[1.Family life—Vietnam. 2. Vietnam—Social life and customs.]
I. Title. II. Series: Families around the world.
HQ674.5.S26 1998
306.85'09597—dc21 97-41240

Contents

★ Introduction

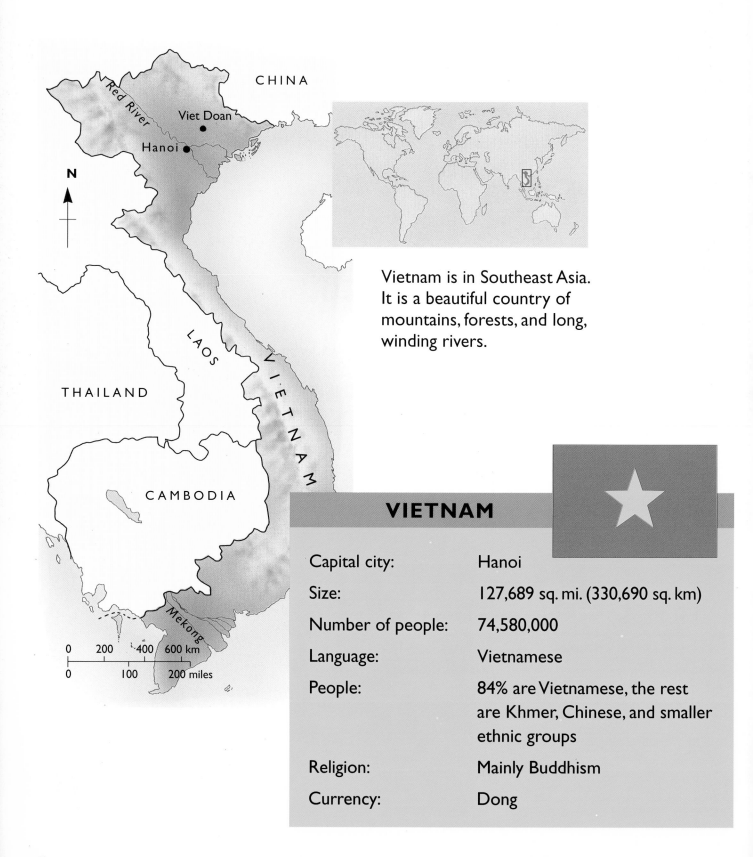

Vietnam is in Southeast Asia. It is a beautiful country of mountains, forests, and long, winding rivers.

VIETNAM

Capital city:	Hanoi
Size:	127,689 sq. mi. (330,690 sq. km)
Number of people:	74,580,000
Language:	Vietnamese
People:	84% are Vietnamese, the rest are Khmer, Chinese, and smaller ethnic groups
Religion:	Mainly Buddhism
Currency:	Dong

THE NGUYEN FAMILY

Size of household:	5 people
Size of home:	860 sq. ft. (80 sq. m)
Workweek:	119 hours (adults)
Most valued possessions:	Ha: His bicycle Hung: His football

Income for each
  family member:
	About $285
	  each year

The Nguyen family is an ordinary Vietnamese family. They have put everything that they own outside their home so that this photograph could be taken.

Meet the Family

1 Ha, father, 33
2 Canh, mother, 31
3 Huong, daughter, 9

4 Hung, son, 7
5 Hai, daughter, 3

WAR IN VIETNAM

In the 1960s and 1970s, people from the north and south of Vietnam fought each other in a terrible war. Many parts of Vietnam were destroyed. The war ended twenty years ago. Now Vietnam is building for the future.

Family Life

The Nguyen family lives in a small village called Viet Doan in the north of Vietnam. Many of their relatives live close by. There are often lots of visitors in the house.

6

Helping Out

The children's grandmother visits the family every day. She knows exactly what to do, because she had ten children of her own. Ha and Canh are happy to have just three children.

"I have five brothers and sisters, and Ha has nine. Today, it is too expensive to have so many children."—*Canh*

At Home

Ha's family have lived in this house for many years.

BUILDING HOUSES

In the countryside, houses are often made from wood, straw, or palm leaves. These materials are cheap because they can be found nearby. Some houses are built on stilts to keep out wild animals or water if there is a flood.

A Family Home

Ha is very proud of his family's house. It was built many years ago by his grandparents. Vietnamese people like to live in the places where their ancestors lived before them. This makes them feel closer to their ancestors.

The house has everything that the family needs. It has one main room and a storage room. The living room is where the family eats, talks, and sleeps. Canh and Ha share one bed with Hai, their younger daughter. It is a tight squeeze, because Hai is growing very quickly. Hung and Huong share the other bed.

Ha helps Huong with her homework at the living-room table.

We have nets around our beds to keep out mosquitoes. They give you nasty bites." — *Hung*

In the Yard

Outside the house, there is a big backyard. There, the family stores hay and keeps some chickens so that there are fresh eggs to eat. Huong and Hung take turns feeding the chickens. The children also like to play in the backyard.

"Sometimes, the chickens creep into the house. Mom is always chasing them outside."—*Huong*

Huong likes to watch the chickens scratching for food in the backyard.

Food and Cooking

Canh puts the food into small bowls and serves the meals on big metal trays.

UNUSUAL DISHES

There are many different kinds of Vietnamese foods, with over 500 interesting dishes to choose from. Some of these dishes are unusual. Some restaurants serve steamed snake and fried gecko, a type of lizard.

In the garden, Ha grows most of the vegetables that his family needs. They do not have a refrigerator, so Canh goes to the market every day to buy food.

12

Cooking Breakfast

Canh makes sure that everyone eats three good meals a day. For breakfast, she cooks a strong, spicy soup called *Pho*. Canh uses the meat juices left over from the night before. Then she adds noodles, vegetables, lime, chilis, and fish sauce.

Canh usually cooks outside in the backyard, where there is plenty of space for all the pots and pans.

Eating Together

At lunchtime and dinnertime Canh puts the food into little plates and bowls. Everyone has a bowl for rice and another one for soup. There is a bowl of water, so that the family can clean their fingers while they are eating. Everyone uses chopsticks to pick up food from the different dishes.

"During the evening meal, we tell the rest of the family about our day."
—*Ha*

"Hai likes to play with the water while she is washing the vegetables."
— *Canh*

"When the children grow up, it will be difficult to squeeze us all in!"—*Ha*

The whole family sits on the floor to eat, which makes it easier to fit everyone in.

Special Occasions

The Nguyens and their relatives always like to eat together on special occasions, such as festivals and public holidays.

On holidays, Canh goes to the market with her mother and sisters. They usually buy chickens or a large fish. The other relatives help by cooking, and everyone shares the dishes they have brought. The children always get excited because the house is full of people talking, laughing, and eating.

"I like chatting to the market traders. I ask them to save the best chickens for me!"—*Canh*

Working Hard

Although Ha works very hard, he makes sure that he spends some time with his children.

GROWING RICE

More than half the people in Vietnam are farmers, and rice is the most important crop. Rice needs lots of water to grow, so farmers dig channels to carry water to their fields. The flooded rice fields are called paddies.

An Early Start

Everyone in the Nguyen family has a job. Hung gets up at five in the morning to feed the chickens. If they have laid any eggs, he gives them to his mother to use in soup. Huong gets her little sister ready for nursery school.

Work in the Fields

Ha and Canh go to work when the sun rises and return home after dark. Canh grows rice with the other villagers. It is very hard work, but they all help each other. Before she plants the rice, Canh uses her neighbor's water buffalo to churn the paddy into a soupy mud. Then she floods the field with water. When the rice is ripe, Canh collects the grains of rice from the plants.

The villagers work together so that everyone can have a good rice harvest.

This machine separates the grains of rice from the rest of the plant.

Supplying Water

Ha works at a pumping station. He has to make sure that the pumps supply enough water to the ditches and canals around the local rice paddies. Ha works very long hours.

Earning Enough

Ha always cycles to work because it is too far to walk.

Ha and Canh make just enough money to keep the family well fed. Sometimes they have a little extra to buy some new clothes or some schoolbooks for the children.

School and Play

Huong helps her mother by taking Hai to the nursery school each day.

EDUCATION

Education is very important in Vietnam. Almost all Vietnamese children can read and write. Even though it is a poor country, many older students save to go to college.

Huong and Hung go to the primary school near their home. Hai has just started going to nursery school. It does not take them long to walk there, but Huong usually gives Hai a ride on her sholders.

"I like walking to school with my friends."—*Hung*

Huong's class has forty children.

After School

Huong works hard at school. She wants to do well in her exams next year and hopes she will get a good job when she is older. Every night Huong spends a long time doing her homework.

Hung does not have to do much homework yet. He can spend more time playing with his friends. Hung loves playing soccer. He also likes collecting insects and racing them against each other.

"One day, I want to be on the Vietnam soccer team—it's one of the best teams in Asia!"—*Hung*

Spare Time

The Nguyens like to spend public holidays with their relatives.

There are many festivals in Vietnam. One of the most important festivals is *Tet*, when Vietnamese people celebrate New Year. People pray in pagodas and prepare special family feasts. They also set off loud firecrackers to celebrate.

Time to Relax

The family does not have much free time, but everyone makes the most of it. Canh practices an ancient Chinese pastime called *Tai ji*. It helps her to stretch all her muscles after a hard day's work. Huong and Hung like to watch television at their uncle's house.

Days Out

Hanoi, the capital city of Vietnam, is only an hour from Viet Doan by bus. On holidays, the Nguyens sometimes go there to see a puppet show. They also like to walk around the beautiful lake in the middle of the city. The adults visit a pagoda to pray.

"Hung is always collecting things! I help him find new bits and pieces."—*Huong*

Hung and Huong spend a lot of time playing together.

The Future

Many Vietnamese people now use motorbikes to get around.

A CHANGING COUNTRY

Until recently, Vietnam was one of the poorest countries in the world. But it is changing very fast. Some farmers are moving to big cities to take up new jobs in factories and hotels. Many foreign businesses are moving to Vietnam, too.

Everyone in the Nguyen family hopes that their lives will be easier in the future. Ha would like to buy a motorbike. Huong wants to become a teacher. If Hung is not good enough to get on the Vietnam soccer team, he hopes to get a job in a new hotel in Hanoi.

"In the past, my country fought many wars. I hope that Vietnam will always be a peaceful place in the future."—*Huong*

Pronunciation Guide

Canh	Kawn	**pagoda**	pah-goe-duh
		pho	foe
Ha	Ah		
Hai	Eye	**Tai ji**	Tie-gee
Hanoi	Han-oye		
Huong	Wong	**Viet Doan**	Vee-et Doe-ann
Hung	Ung		
Khmer	Cuh-mare		
Nguyen	Un-goo-wen		

Glossary

Ancestors Members of a family who lived and died many years ago.

Buddhim Religious beliefs developed by Buddha, a religious leader from India.

Chilis Small, very spicy vegetables.

Chopsticks A pair of thin sticks that people use to pick up food.

Ethnic group People who share the same language, religion, and traditions.

Independent To be free from the control of other countries.

Khmer People who come from Cambodia, a country near Vietnam, in Southeast Asia.

Mosquitoes Small insects that bite.

Noodles A dried food, made from flour, and into thin strips.

Pagodas Buildings where people go to worship.

Pumping station A building in which pumps are set up to move water from one place to another.

Stilts Long posts that are used to raise buildings off the ground.

Tai ji An ancient exercise that is meant to help the body and mind.

Water buffalo A large, strong animal from southern Asia. It is a bit like a cow.

Books to Read

Brown, Tricia. *The Story of a Vietnamese-American Girl*. New York: Putnam Publishing Group, 1991.

Geography Department Staff. *Vietnam In Pictures* (Visual Geography Series). Minneapolis, MN: Lerner Publications, 1994.

Hansen, Ole Steen. *Vietnam* (Economically Developing Countries). Austin, TX: Raintree Steck-Vaughn, 1997.

Mathews, Jo. *I Remember Vietnam* (Why We Left). Austin, TX: Raintree Steck-Vaughn, 1994.

Parker, Lewis K. *Vietnam* (Dropping In On). Vero Beach, FL: Rourke Book Co., 1994.

Index